Sendi Lee Mason
AND THE GREAT CRUSADE

Sendi Lee Mason and the Great Crusade.

Copyright © 1991 by Hilda Stahl.

Published by Crossway Books, a division of
Good News Publishers, Wheaton, Illinois 60187.

Series design: Ad Plus; Cover illustration: Deborah Huffman

First printing, 1991

Printed in the United States of America

ISBN 0-89107-632-8

99		98		97		96		95		94		93		92		91
15	14	13	12	11	10	9	8	7	6	5	4	3	2	1

Dedicated with love to
Benjamin Stahl

A GROWING UP ADVENTURE

Sendi Lee Mason

AND THE
GREAT CRUSADE

Hilda Stahl

CROSSWAY BOOKS • WHEATON, ILLINOIS
A DIVISION OF GOOD NEWS PUBLISHERS

Contents

1 The Snowman Family   9

2 English Assignment   19

3 The Big Lie   29

4 Lee Reins   37

5 The Surprise   51

6 Christmas Shopping   61

7 A Talk with Pine   75

8 Diane   87

9 A Family Christmas   97

10 A Real Family   115

1

The Snowman Family

Sendi set her bright red hat on the small snowman's head. She stepped back and laughed right out loud. Her fingers tingled with cold. Her breath hung in the air. But she didn't care. She had built the perfect snowman family.

Sendi touched the tall dad. "You're Lee Reins. You're my dad." Sendi touched the medium-sized mom. "You're Janice Mason. My mom." Sendi touched the small child. "And you're me! Sendi Lee Mason." She laughed again. "We are a family."

Just then Gwen McNeeley, Sendi's very best friend, ran from her house next door to Sendi's snowy yard. Gwen's brown eyes brimmed with tears. Her green and yellow jacket was unzipped. She didn't have on a hat or mittens. "Sendi, I am devastated!"

Sendi's stomach knotted. Sometimes she didn't know what Gwen was saying. Gwen's parents were high school English teachers, and Gwen was their only child. They taught her much more than most

nine-year-olds knew. "Did you hurt yourself, Gwen?"

Gwen shook her head and her long,
brown hair flipped around her thin
shoulders.

"Did Mrs. Lewis yell at you?" Sendi
looked toward Gwen's house. Mrs.
Lewis took care of Gwen. "Did Mrs.
Lewis make you eat a carrot?" Sendi
knew Gwen hated carrots.

Gwen knuckled away her tears and
shook her head. "I just realized I have
no great mission in life."

"You still look at milk cartons to see
if you know the missing kids," said
Sendi.

"I know," said Gwen with a sigh.

"You still tell kids to say no to
drugs," said Sendi.

Gwen sighed again. "I know."

"And you still see that the neighbor-
hood recycles," said Sendi.

Gwen nodded. She spread her arms wide. "But I don't have any new mission!"

Sendi looked away from Gwen at her snowman family. Suddenly she had a *great* idea. It amazed her. "Gwen, I have a great mission in life," whispered Sendi. She thought if she said it too loud, the idea would disappear.

Gwen frowned. "You never have a great mission in life."

"I do now," said Sendi.

"What is it?" asked Gwen.

"See my snowman family?" Sendi lovingly touched each one of them.

Gwen nodded. "They're cute. You could even win a contest with them. I like the noses even if they are carrots."

Sendi stepped close to Gwen. "My great mission in life is to have Lee and Mom get married so we can be a real family."

Gwen's eyes widened. "That's awesome! That's more than a great mission. That's a great crusade!"

Sendi swelled with pride.

Suddenly Gwen's face fell, and she looked ready to cry "What about me? How can I survive if I don't have a great mission? You have a great crusade, and I have nothing!"

"You can help me," said Sendi with a smile.

Gwen sighed and nodded. "I will help you because we are best friends. But it's just not the same, Sendi. You can't understand because you've never had a mission before. I am devastated! I am in the depths of despair! How can I face anyone after this?"

Sendi didn't know what to say. "Don't be upset, Gwen. You'll think of a mission. You always do." Ever since Sendi had moved next door to Gwen last summer, Gwen had had a great mission in life. Her parents had helped her in any way they could.

Sendi didn't have two parents. She only had a mom. Mom was a hair stylist at Hair Care, so she usually wasn't around even if Sendi had had a great mission in life. Mom couldn't afford a baby-sitter, so Sendi was alone every afternoon after school until Mom got home. "Please, don't cry, Gwen."

"I won't." Gwen swallowed hard. "I think my tears are turning to icicles on my face."

"What can I do to make Mom and Lee want to get married so we can be a family?" asked Sendi.

"I don't know," said Gwen.

Sendi stared at Gwen in shock. Gwen always knew everything!

"You'll think of something," said

Gwen. She shivered. "I've got to get home before I freeze into a popsicle."

Frowning, Sendi watched Gwen run to her house. She slammed her door hard enough to knock an icicle off the roof. It shattered as it hit the ground.

Sendi turned back to her snowman family. She touched the dad, the mom, and the child. If they could talk, would they tell her how to make Lee, Mom, and her into a happy family?

Suddenly Sendi had a brilliant idea! She laughed and hugged the dad snowman. She would leave her wonderful snowman family here in the front yard for Mom and Lee to see! It would make them think about becoming a family!

Lee Reinswas her real father, but he hadn't known about Sendi until Mom wrote and told him several weeks ago. He'd come from Oklahoma to meet Sendi and then decided to stay. He said

God wanted him to live near Sendi instead of in Oklahoma.

Sendi hugged the dad snowman again. Mom and Lee would get married, and the three of them would live happily ever after!

Just then Diane Roscommon ran into Sendi's yard. "Did you finish the English homework?" asked Diane, flipping back her long, light brown hair.

Sendi shook her head. "I wanted to build my snowman family first. Isn't this a nice family?"

Diane frowned at her. She had two brothers older than her and two sisters younger. Diane said she felt like a thin layer of peanut butter between two thick slices of bread. "You need more kids in it."

"But it's my family." Sendi touched each snowman. "This is my dad and my mom and me."

Diane tipped back her head and laughed loudly enough for everyone on the block to hear. "That's dumb! Lee Reins will never marry your mom! She's too fat!"

Sendi's cheeks burned, and sparks flew from her blue eyes. "Lee Reins is my dad! And he will too marry my mom! And we will be a family!"

Diane shook her head. "You'll never be a real family. So there!"

"We will too!" cried Sendi. Tears burned her eyes, but she would not cry in front of Diane.

Suddenly Diane kicked the child snowman, scattering it across the small front yard. Sendi's red hat fell to the snowy ground.

Blood roared in Sendi's ears. "Stop that!"

Diane lunged against the mom snowman and knocked it flat. She knocked the head off the dad snowman. She turned to Sendi. "Now you don't even have a snowman family!"

Sendi burst into tears and ran to the shoebox-sized house where she and Mom lived.

"You'll never have a real family, Sendi Mason!" shouted Diane.

Sendi burst into the house and slammed the door hard behind her. The heat inside rushed at her and burned into her. She leaned against the door as tears streamed down her icy cheeks. Was Diane right?

2

English Assignment

Sobbing harder, Sendi dropped her jacket and mittens in a heap on the living room floor. She jerked off her boots, sending snow skittering across the thin, faded carpet.

Just then Diane opened the door and stuck her head inside. "Sendi, I'm sorry for wrecking your snowman family."

Sendi knotted her fists at her sides. Diane always did naughty things, then said she was sorry. Well, this time Sendi would not forgive her! "Get out of my house!" yelled Sendi.

Diane stepped all the way in and shut the door. "But I need your help with my English assignment."

Sendi stamped her foot. "Go away!"

Diane shook her head. "You can't make me. I said I was sorry. I said I need help. Why won't you help me?"

Sendi shook her finger at Diane. "You . . . you were mean to me!"

"I said I was sorry!" cried Diane.

Sendi narrowed her eyes and glared at Diane. "I won't help you."

"Then it'll be your fault if I fail

English." Diane tossed back her long hair. "I have to write my favorite Christmas memory. How do I know what it is?"

"Get out of my house right now!" Sendi jerked open the door. Cold air rushed in and she shivered. "Get out now!"

Diane pressed her lips tightly together and stomped out the door. Sendi slammed it after her.

She walked behind the ugly orange and brown flowered chair that matched the ugly orange and brown flowered sofa. She paused at the kitchen doorway, then paced by her bedroom door. She punched the back of the ugly orange and brown chair. She didn't know what she'd write in her report either. Maybe she could make up a favorite memory of Mom, Lee, and herself having Christmas together. That made her think of her great crusade. She wouldn't tell Diane about it. Diane would tell everyone, and then laugh and laugh.

Just then someone knocked on the door. Sendi frowned. Was it Diane again?

Sendi ran to the door and jerked it open. Pine Cordell, the old ex-cowboy from Wyoming, stood there. He held Sendi's black and white kitten in his gloved hand. He lived three houses away and took care of Baby while Sendi was in school.

"You forgot to pick up Baby," said Pine, setting the kitten on the floor. She immediately rubbed against Sendi's ankle and then ran to the kitchen to her special dish. Pine patted Sendi's shoulder. "Is something wrong, little friend?"

"Diane knocked down my snowman family!" said Sendi with a sniff.

"I'm sure sorry, Sendi," said Pine as he pushed his cowboy hat to the back of his bald head. "Diane sometimes forgets to act like Jesus wants her to."

"She sure does!" Sendi nodded hard.

"You just keep lovin' her like Jesus does," said Pine with a smile that showed off his chipped front tooth.

Sendi looked down at her stocking feet. She would not love Diane!

"See you in the mornin'," said Pine, stepping back outdoors.

Sendi nodded. She always dropped Baby off at Pine's house on her way to school. She watched Pine walk down the sidewalk. Then she saw the scattered pieces of her snowman family, and fresh anger roared through her. She slammed the door with a bang. Diane would be very, very sorry for what she had done!

Several minutes later Janice drove her old blue Chevy into the driveway. Sendi watched her get out of the car and walk slowly to the house. Her shoulder-length blonde hair was in perfect order.

Sendi opened the door. "Hi, Mom."

"Hi, Sendi." Janice slowly hung up her coat. "I'm tired to the bone, Sendi." She sank to the sofa. Long, red earrings danced on her plump shoulders. Her red, blue, green, and gray flowered big shirt hung over her blue slacks. She kicked off her shoes and curled up on the sofa.

"Is Lee coming over tonight, Mom?" asked Sendi as she perched on the edge of the big chair.

"He might," said Janice. "Why?"

Sendi shrugged. "I just want to see him."

"He's very busy now that he's teach-

ing math at the middle school and try-
ing to find an apartment."

"Why can't he move in with us?"

Janice frowned. "Because we're not
married."

"You could get married," said Sendi.
Her heart stood still as she waited for
Mom's answer.

"It's not that simple, Sendi." Janice
pushed herself up. "I guess I should
make supper. Are you very hungry?"

"Doesn't he love you?" asked Sendi
around the hard lump in her throat.

"Not enough to marry me," said
Janice, looking sad.

"He loved you once," said Sendi.

"That was a long time ago when we
were kids. Then his parents moved to
Oklahoma, and he had to go with them.
So he stopped loving me."

"And you got mad at him because

you were going to have me, so you stopped loving him," said Sendi.

Janice sighed loud and long. "Lee and I sinned against God and against each other, Sendi. I explained all of that to you. But we asked Jesus to forgive us, and He did."

"Lee's here now, and you can love each other again," said Sendi.

"I don't want to talk about it," said Janice sharply.

"You can marry Lee. Then I can call him Dad," said Sendi.

Janice brushed a tear off her long lashes. "You can call him Dad now."

"Dad." Sendi rolled the word around on her tongue. It felt good to say it.

"Did you do your homework, Sendi?" asked Janice as she walked to the kitchen.

"Not yet."

Janice frowned over her shoulder at Sendi. "Get to it."

Sendi ran to her tiny bedroom and picked up the paper she'd dropped on her bed. "MY FAVORITE CHRISTMAS MEMORY" was written in bold letters across the top of the blank page. She had to fill the whole page with her favorite Christmas memory. For all the Christmases she could remember she and Mom had lived with Momma in her big white house. Momma was Mom's mother, but Sendi had always called her Momma because Mom did. Every year it had been the three of them around a tiny Christmas tree to open presents and then at the table to eat their Christmas dinner. There was no special memory worth writing about.

Suddenly Sendi held the paper to her heart, and her pulse leaped. She'd write what she wanted this Christmas to be! She would write that she and Mom and Lee were a real family living together. They'd have a real Christmas tree, presents, and everything!

She sat cross-legged on her bed, put her paper on her book, and printed her report neatly and quickly. When she finished, she read it over, smiled, then held it against her heart. She would convince Mom and Lee to get married! They'd be a real family. "A real family," Sendi whispered in awe.

3

The Big Lie

Sendi gripped her English paper tight as she hung her jacket and hat on the hook outside the fourth grade room. Other fourth graders crowded around the racks, laughing and talking. Smells of wet wool and coffee from the teachers' lounge filled the noisy hallway.

Sendi smiled down at her paper. Maybe writing down her dream Christmas would make it come true. What would Miss Taylor say about her report?

"Sendi!" cried Diane, gripping Sendi's arm. "You've got to read my paper!"

Sendi jerked away from Diane. "No way!"

Diane shook the paper under Sendi's nose. "I wrote about the time I thought I got a real baby for Christmas, but it was my new baby sister."

"I don't want to read it," said Sendi, stepping back and frowning.

"It might be too dumb to hand in," said Diane, sounding close to tears.

"It probably is," said Sendi.

Diane stared at Sendi in shock. "Are you still mad at me?"

"I will stay mad at you forever!" snapped Sendi. She pushed Diane aside and strode into the fourth grade room.

Sendi took a deep breath and looked around. She saw Gwen already at her desk, her head down. Sendi knew Gwen was still upset because she didn't have a great mission in life.

Slowly Sendi walked to Miss Taylor's desk. Sendi's stomach tightened. Should she hand in her paper? What if Miss Taylor read it aloud for all to hear?

Miss Taylor looked up with a smile. Her mass of curly black hair streamed down over her slender shoulders and back. "Good morning, Sendi."

"Here's my English paper," said Sendi just above a whisper.

Miss Taylor took the paper and laid it in a red in-basket at the corner of her desk.

Sendi just stood there. She moved

from one foot to the other. Her pink
sweater suddenly felt too hot.

"Did you want something, Sendi?"
asked Miss Taylor, pushing the sleeves
of her red sweater almost to her elbows.
Gold bracelets clinked on her wrist. The
sweet smell of perfume drifted around
her.

Sendi swallowed hard. "Miss Taylor,
please don't read my paper out loud,"
whispered Sendi.

Miss Taylor patted Sendi's arm. "I
won't if you don't want me to."

"Thank you." Sendi managed a
smile and then walked to her desk. She
looked at Gwen, but her head was still
down.

"Did you hand in your paper,
Gwen?" whispered Sendi.

"Of course," said Gwen without
looking up.

"How long are you going to be sad?" asked Sendi.

Gwen looked at her with tears filling her eyes. "Until I'm old and gray like Mrs. Lewis. I'll rock in my chair and watch TV and crochet just like Mrs. Lewis does. Having no mission in life is the worst thing that ever happened to me."

"I'm sorry, Gwen," said Sendi. She thought about her great crusade and smiled.

Later in the morning Miss Taylor said, "It's time to hand in your English assignment if you haven't done so yet."

Three boys carried their papers to the desk and dropped them in the basket. They ran to their seats, pushing and shoving each other.

Miss Taylor looked over the papers. "Diane, please hand your assignment in."

Diane rattled papers in her desk. "I can't find it, Miss Taylor."

Sendi moved restlessly. "Diane, you know the paper is due," said Miss Taylor impatiently. "Did you leave it in your jacket pocket?"

"No." Diane looked through her messy desk again. "I lost it!"

"Diane!" Miss Taylor walked around her desk and stood with her hands at her waist. She frowned at Diane. "Did you even do your lesson?"

"Yes!" cried Diane. "Ask Sendi Mason. She saw it."

Sendi sank low in her desk. She hated to have everyone look at her.

Miss Taylor crossed her arms. "Sendi, did you see Diane's paper?"

Sendi looked at Diane. Her eyes were wide and pleading. Just then Sendi thought of her snowman family that Diane had knocked down. Sendi thought of all the bad things Diane had done to her. Slowly Sendi turned to Miss Taylor. "I never saw Diane's paper."

"Sendi Mason!" cried Diane. "That's a big lie!"

Sendi's face flamed. How could she lie? It was wrong!

"Diane!" snapped Miss Taylor. "Don't make matters worse."

"Sendi does not lie," said Gwen.

Sendi's heart turned over. A black cloud settled over her. She glanced at Gwen, then at Diane.

"Please, Sendi," said Diane in a low, tight voice.

"You get an automatic failure for the day without the paper," said Miss Taylor. "I told you that yesterday."

Diane's eyes filled with tears. "I did write my report! And Sendi knows I did!"

Sendi locked her icy hands together in her lap. She had lied, but she didn't care! Diane deserved a failure for the day. She deserved worse than that!

A great sadness rose up inside Sendi, but she wouldn't tell Miss Taylor the truth.

"I'll read two of the papers," said Miss Taylor. "If you don't want yours read, please let me know."

Sendi glanced around. Two boys and one girl raised their hands. She felt better knowing she wasn't the only one who didn't want hers read.

Sendi glanced at Diane. Diane stuck her tongue out at Sendi. Sendi quickly looked at Miss Taylor. Sendi tried to listen to the first paper, but she couldn't hear a word. Her head buzzed with the terrible lie she'd told. She sat up straighter and let it buzz.

4

Lee Reins

After school Sendi ran down the side-walk toward home. Chilly wind blew against her, and she huddled down into her jacket. Gwen had a piano lesson. It was the only day they didn't walk home together. Sendi waited at the corner for several cars to pass. Snow sparkled like diamonds in the sunlight. Her face tingled with cold. Would it be fun to take piano lessons? Maybe Lee Reins would love her more if she could play the piano. He was coming for supper tonight. She'd ask him if he wanted her to learn piano. "I wish I could ask him to marry Mom," Sendi muttered.

Suddenly a snowball spattered against Sendi's back. She spun around. Diane stood several feet away, a pleased look on her flushed face. She wore a bright pink jacket with a fluffy white hat and mittens.

"That's for telling a lie," said Diane.

Sendi scooped up a handful of snow and threw it at Diane. Diane jumped aside, and the snowball flew past.

"I found my English paper and handed it in," said Diane, running up to Sendi. "I'm not mad anymore. Are you?"

"Yes! I will stay mad forever!"

snapped Sendi, slapping the snow off her mittens.

Diane's face fell. "I guess you won't let me ride your bike anymore."

"You can't even look at it!" Sendi ran down the sidewalk to get away from Diane. Sendi listened, but didn't hear anyone following her. She glanced over her shoulder. Diane was walking slowly, her head down. "I hope she never speaks to me again," muttered Sendi.

A few minutes later Sendi stopped at Pine's for Baby. Pine stood in the yard, looking at his bird feeder. Sendi didn't want to stay to talk today. Pine seemed to be able to see right inside her and know what she was thinking and feeling. She didn't want him to know what she'd done to Diane.

"Aren't the birds beautiful, Sendi?" said Pine, smiling at her. "I saw a cardinal this morning. That bright red against the white snow is a thing of beauty."

Sendi managed to smile. "Is Baby in the house?"

"Sure is. Cats and birds don't mix." Pine chuckled.

"Like some folks I know."

Sendi looked at him sharply. Did he mean her and Diane?

"Just think of how God takes care of the birds!" Pine folded his arms over his sheepskin-lined coat. "Birds don't have to work for a living. God provides for them. He made them for us to enjoy. He loves us, Sendi, and don't ever forget it!"

"I won't," Sendi said. But she didn't want to think about God loving her. If she thought too much about God, she'd have to stop being mad at Diane.

Pine opened his door and called, "Baby! Sendi's here to get you."

Baby mewed and ran to Pine. He scooped her up and handed her to Sendi. Baby felt warm and soft in Sendi's hands.

"Thank you, Pine," said Sendi. "I'll see you in the morning."

"Be sure to bring a can of cat food," said Pine. "I'm all out."

"I will." Sendi walked slowly home, Baby against her heart. Saturday afternoons Sendi worked for Mrs. Wells at the corner grocery store to earn enough to buy cat food and kitty litter. Janice didn't make enough money to take care of Baby. So, for Sendi to get a kitten, she'd had to find a way to earn money. Sendi kept a box of kitty litter at her house, and Pine kept a box at his house. She made sure he always had cat food for Baby. Sometimes Sendi got tired of delivering groceries and sweeping the floor at the store. Then she'd think about how much she loved Baby, and she gladly went to work.

Later in her house Sendi stood in the bathroom doorway. Mom had asked her to clean the bathroom and her bedroom.

"We want everything nice and clean when Lee comes," Janice had said this morning before she'd gone to work.

Sendi hated cleaning, especially the bathroom, but she wanted everything perfect for Lee's visit. "I'll clean my bedroom first," she muttered.

She stepped inside her tiny room. There was room for a dresser and a bed. A pile of clothes lay on the floor of the closet. Her bed was unmade, and her coloring books and other books were scattered across the floor. Sendi touched her birth certificate hanging on the wall near the light switch. It said "Father Unknown" on it. Should she hide it in her dresser drawer so Lee couldn't see it and feel bad? She nodded as she lifted it off the nail. She looked at her name, "SENDI LEE MASON." Mom hadn't known how to spell very well. She'd wanted to name her baby girl Cindy, so she thought it would be *S*E*N*D* with an *I* added to it. Sendi always had to tell each new teacher why her name was spelled the way it was. But she liked telling the story. She liked best to hear Mom tell it. With a smile Sendi stuck her birth certificate in her drawer.

Just then she heard Diane shouting at the neighbor boys. Sendi covered her ears. She didn't want to hear Diane or think about what she'd done to her. Finally she took her hands off her ears. All she heard was the furnace humming.

Sendi kept busy until Janice came home from work. Janice was flushed as she hurried to the kitchen with a bag of groceries. She smelled like a new perm.

"Lee likes spaghetti and meatballs," said Janice. "I'll have garlic bread and a salad too."

Sendi's heart leaped just at seeing Mom's glowing face. "Mom, I know you love Lee! I know you want to marry him!"

Janice whirled on Sendi and shook her finger at her. "Don't you dare say that to Lee! I mean it, Sendi Lee Mason!"

Sendi giggled. "I won't, Mom."

A few minutes later someone knocked, and Sendi ran to the door. She was sure it was Lee even though it was a little early. Sendi flung the door wide, and then her smile faded. It was Diane.

"Can I borrow your box of magic markers, Sendi?" asked Diane. "I have to use them for a map for social studies."

"No!" Sendi slammed the door.

"What in the world is wrong with

you, Sendi?" asked Janice from the kitchen doorway.

Sendi flushed. "I don't want Diane to use my markers."

"Why not? Open that door and call her back right now!" said Janice firmly.

Sendi hesitated, then opened the door. Diane was almost in her yard. "Come back, Diane," called Sendi. "You can use my markers."

Diane shouted happily as she ran through the snow to Sendi. "I knew you couldn't stay mad forever."

Sendi clamped her lips tightly closed as she led Diane to her bedroom. She pushed the box of markers into Diane's hand. "Mom made me do this," whispered Sendi. "I didn't want to. Don't you dare lose them!"

"I won't," said Diane. She walked to the door, then smiled at Sendi. "I'm going to be nice to you from now on."

Sendi rolled her eyes. Diane always said that, but she still did naughty things when she felt like it.

Sendi opened the door, and cold air rushed in. As Diane walked out, Lee came up the sidewalk. If the snowman family were still standing, Lee would see it and want to become a real family. Fresh anger at Diane rushed through Sendi.

"Hi, Diane," Lee said.

"Hi," said Diane with a wide smile. "Sendi's mad at me. But I am being nice to her anyway."

Sendi flushed. Couldn't Diane ever keep her big mouth shut?

Lee stepped inside, and Sendi closed the door against the cold air. Lee brushed back his blond hair and then hung his leather jacket in the closet. He wore a western blue plaid shirt, Levis, and black cowboy boots. He hugged Sendi close. "How's my girl?"

"Fine," she said. She liked the smell of his after-shave.

"Hi, Lee," said Janice, stepping forward. She'd changed into a rose-colored shirt and pants.

Lee hugged Janice. "I'm glad to see you." Sendi locked her hands over her heart and beamed. Lee wouldn't hug Mom if he didn't love her a little, surely.

Janice flushed. "I'm making spaghetti."

"Good. Anything I can do to help?" asked Lee.

Janice shook her head, sending her gold hoop earrings dancing. "Maybe you could check over Sendi's homework to see if she finished it."

"Will do," said Lee, catching Sendi's hand. "Let's see it, Sendi."

Sendi gasped. "I forgot to do it! But I'll do it now."

"I think you'd better," said Janice sharply.

"I want to have a little talk with you first," said Lee, tugging Sendi to the ugly sofa.

"I'll let you two talk," said Janice, smiling at them before she walked to the kitchen.

Sendi's stomach tightened. She sat on the edge of the sofa as she listened to Mom humming in the kitchen. Sendi couldn't look at Lee.

Lee turned Sendi toward him. "Now, suppose you tell me why you're mad at Diane?"

Sendi frantically searched for an answer. She couldn't tell Lee the real reason. "Diane's always doing bad things to me," Sendi finally said.

"I know, but you must forgive her," said Lee. "Jesus said you must forgive over and over and over."

"I know," said Sendi weakly.

"Jesus wants you to forgive Diane," said Lee. "I do too."

Sendi sighed heavily. She did not want to forgive Diane. But she couldn't tell Lee that. She'd have to tell him what he wanted to hear. Sendi looked down at the pearl snaps on Lee's shirt. "I will forgive Diane," she said just above a whisper. The lie burned her throat.

"That's my girl!" Lee hugged Sendi tight. "You go do your homework, and I'll check it later."

Sendi ran to her room and hunted for her social studies worksheet. She'd finished the map, but she still had a few questions to answer.

A few minutes later she heard Mom join Lee on the sofa. Sendi peeked through the door and watched them sitting side by side. How wonderful it would be if they got married!

"Can you come again tomorrow?" asked Janice softly.

Sendi held her breath for Lee's answer.

"I made other plans," Lee said. He cleared his throat. "I might as well tell you, Janice."

"What?" she asked in a small voice.

Sendi tensed.

"I'm taking Lorna Roberts out for dinner," said Lee.

Sendi fell back, her face pale.

Janice jumped up. "I'd better see if the water's boiling yet." She sounded ready to cry.

Sendi slumped to her bed. Lee was taking Lorna Roberts out! Oh, what if he married Lorna instead of Mom?

5

The Surprise

Sendi forced down another bite of spaghetti. Neither Mom nor Lee were eating much either.

"I found a place to live finally," said Lee as he wiped his mouth with a white paper napkin.

"Where?" asked Janice. She didn't

look at Lee, but studied her glass of water as if she saw something strange on the ice cube.

Sendi hoped Lee lived a long way from Lorna Roberts.

Lee laughed. "You'll never guess."

Janice looked at him with a slight frown. "Just tell us, Lee," she said impatiently.

"With Pine Cordell," said Lee smugly.

Sendi clapped her hands and laughed.

"With Pine?" asked Janice, smiling hesitantly.

"Only three houses away," said Lee. He leaned his elbows on the table and folded his hands. "I told Pine I was looking for a place to live, and he said he had a spare room if I was interested. He said it'd help with his expenses and would be nice for me to be so close to the two of you."

"It's great!" cried Sendi.

"I can be with you after school until your mom gets home," said Lee, smiling at Sendi.

"That's not necessary," said Janice stiffly.

"I want to," said Lee.

"Are you saying I'm not a good mother?" asked Janice.

"Not at all!" Lee shook his head. "I just want to do this, Janice."

"All right." Janice nodded, but she didn't look very happy.

Lee tugged Sendi's hair. "How about running over to Gwen's awhile to give your mom and me a chance to talk."

Sendi slowly stood. Butterflies fluttered in her stomach. "You won't go back to Oklahoma, will you?"

"No, I'm here to stay," said Lee with a smile that didn't reach his eyes.

Hesitantly Sendi walked out of the kitchen. Slowly she slipped on her jacket.

"What about Lorna Roberts?" Sendi heard Mom ask in a low voice.

"I do have a life of my own, Janice," Lee said just as low, but Sendi heard him too.

Sendi wanted to stay to listen, but she knew they wouldn't let her. She walked outdoors and shivered as the cold wind struck her. She felt as cold on the inside as on the outside. The street lights lit the yards. Music drifted out from the Roscommons' house. With her head down, Sendi walked to Gwen's house and knocked on her door.

Gwen opened the door. Heat rushed out along with the smell of baked fish. "Hi, Sendi," Gwen said in surprise as she let Sendi in. "I thought you couldn't come over because your dad was at your place."

Sendi blinked back tears. "They want to talk in private."

"My mom and dad do that all the time," said Gwen, rolling her eyes. She led Sendi to her bedroom. Camille, Gwen's long-haired white cat, jumped from Gwen's bed to her thick blue carpet and rubbed against Sendi's ankle.

Sendi patted Camille and then dropped her jacket at the foot of Gwen's wide bed. The bed, dresser, desk, and bookshelf that held toys and books took up so much room that there wasn't much floor space. Sendi swallowed hard. "Lee's going out to dinner with Lorna Roberts tomorrow night."

"Who's she?" asked Gwen as she picked up a stuffed rabbit and dropped it in place on her pillow.

"A secretary at the middle school," said Sendi, sinking to the plush blue carpet. She leaned against the bed.

"She's probably just a friend," said Gwen. She sat cross-legged in front of Sendi. Camille settled across Gwen's legs and purred loudly.

"My mom's really upset," said Sendi.

"Maybe it is serious," said Gwen.

"What if he marries her?" asked Sendi around the hard lump in her throat.

"That would be awful for you!" cried Gwen. "You have to think of some way to keep that from happening."

Sendi flung her arms wide. "I don't know what to do! I'm not used to making plans and things. Can you think of something, Gwen?"

Gwen sighed heavily. "If I weren't so devastated about my lack of a mission, I could." Suddenly Gwen jumped up, spilling Camille to the floor. "Sendi, I can't believe I didn't think of this before!"

"What?" cried Sendi, leaping to her feet. She just knew Gwen had a great plan.

"Sendi, you are my very best friend, aren't you?"

"Yes."

Gwen tapped her chest. "I will put aside my despair and think about you! I will help you! Mom says that's what Jesus wants us to do, so that's what I'll do."

Sendi sank to the edge of the bed. She couldn't think about what Jesus wanted.

Gwen nodded and her eyes sparkled. "This is really great! I should've thought of it sooner."

"Do you have a plan?" asked Sendi.

"Not yet. But I will!" Laughing, Gwen twirled around the room.

Suddenly she dropped beside Sendi. "The first thing to do is pray. I always pray about my great missions. Have you prayed about yours?"

Sendi's stomach knotted. How could she pray when she was so bad? But she couldn't let Gwen know that! Sendi nodded slightly. "I prayed," she whispered. The words mocked her, but she wouldn't take them back.

"Good! Jesus answers prayer, Sendi. But you know that already, don't you?"

Sendi couldn't nod, but Gwen didn't seem to notice. She kept on talking about the times she'd prayed, and the Lord had answered. Sendi pulled Camille onto her lap and stroked her white fur while Camille purred and Gwen talked.

Later Sendi walked home. Snow swirled in the air and landed on her tangled blonde hair. She reached for the doorknob and sighed heavily. She still didn't have a plan.

Sendi walked in through the back door. The house seemed very quiet. The smell of garlic bread and spaghetti sauce hung in the air. Sendi stopped short as shivers ran up and down her spine. "Mom," called Sendi.

"I'm in here," called Janice. Her voice sounded muffled.

Sendi ran through the living room, dropping her jacket on the ugly sofa. She stopped in the doorway of Mom's tidy bedroom. Mom was lying across the bed. "Where's Lee?" asked Sendi sharply.

Janice pushed herself up and wiped tears from her eyes and blew her nose. She balled the tissue in her hand as she stared down at the thin carpet on the floor. "We had a big fight, and he left."

Sendi gasped. "Left? For good?"

"Maybe," whispered Janice.

"Oh, no!" cried Sendi. "Did he go to Oklahoma?"

Janice shook her head. "To Pine's. He said he'd see you tomorrow."

Sendi sagged weakly against the door frame.

"I told him I don't want to see him again," said Janice.

"What?" cried Sendi.

"You can see him anytime you want, but I don't want to." Janice ran to the bathroom and slammed the door.

Sendi slowly walked to the ugly sofa and sat down. She felt as if someone had kicked all of them down just as Diane had kicked down the snowman family.

Baby mewed, and Sendi picked her up and held her close.

6

Christmas Shopping

The next afternoon Sendi walked into the mall beside Lee. Sendi tried to feel happy about shopping with her very own dad, but she couldn't. She stopped short near the giant water fountain. The noise of the water and the voices of the shoppers echoed down the wide hall-way. A giant Christmas tree stood in the center aisle with giant gifts tucked up under it. Christmas music drifted out from a music store. Sendi looked up at Lee. "It's not right for you to be mad at Mom," said Sendi.

Lee bent down to Sendi. His blue eyes were serious. "I already tried to explain, Sendi. I want my life the way I want it, and your mom wants something different. Now, let's not say another word about your mom, and let's enjoy our shopping trip."

"I thought you were taking Lorna Roberts out to dinner tonight," said Sendi stiffly.

Lee sighed. "I am. But I have time to help you buy a gift for your grandma."

"It might take a long time. I don't know what to buy her," said Sendi.

"Why are you acting this way, Sendi?" asked Lee with a frown.

She wanted to say, "Because I want our family to shop together." Instead she said, "I don't know."

"I think your grandma would like a pair of pink fuzzy slippers," said Lee. "She used to wear some like that all the time. Does she still?"

"Yes," said Sendi as she fell into step beside Lee.

"Your mom says your grandma's coming for Christmas," said Lee.

"I know," said Sendi. She wanted to feel excited about seeing Momma again, but she couldn't. "Will you have Christmas with us?"

"I don't know," said Lee as he walked into Penney's. "I might have other plans."

Suddenly Sendi burst into tears.

She tried to stop crying, but she couldn't.

"Sendi!" Lee gathered her close and led her back out of Penney's to a wooden bench. "What's wrong, honey?"

Sendi clung to Lee. Her shoulders shook with sobs. "Tell me what's wrong, honey."

Sendi finally managed to whisper, "I want you to be with us for Christmas."

"If you feel so strongly about it, then I will come for Christmas. If your mom will let me." Lee wiped Sendi's tears off her ashen cheeks.

"She'll let you!" said Sendi. But would she? Sendi decided that she'd find a way to convince Mom to let Lee come. Sendi hadn't meant to cry, but she had. And her tears had made Lee do what she wanted. She knew tears wouldn't work with Mom. What would? Maybe if Lee said he wouldn't go out with Lorna Roberts ever again, Mom would let him come.

Lee kissed Sendi's cheek. "Let's go buy those slippers for your grandma. I don't have much time left."

Sendi walked into Penney's with Lee. Maybe if she cried hard enough, he wouldn't go to dinner with Lorna Roberts. Sendi tried to squeeze out a tear, but not a one would fall. They bought the fuzzy pink slippers. Sendi tried harder to cry, but she couldn't manage a single sob.

Later Lee dropped Sendi at her house. "I'll see you tomorrow, Sendi," Lee said.

Sendi nodded as she clutched the bag to her.

"I'm glad we could shop together," said Lee.

"Me too," whispered Sendi.

"Please cheer up, Sendi. I love you!"

Lee kissed Sendi's cheek and then ran
back to his car and drove away.

Sendi started toward her front door
when Diane ran to meet her.

"What's in the bag?" asked Diane,
grabbing it. Diane looked inside. "Fuzzy
pink slippers! Are these for your mom?"

Sendi grabbed them back. "For
Momma. I mean, my grandma."

"They're ugly," said Diane.

"They are not!" cried Sendi.

"Here are your markers back," said
Diane, holding them out to Sendi. "I
used up the black."

"Then you'll have to buy me a new
one!" Sendi narrowed her eyes and
glared at Diane. "I use black the most!"

"Get Santa Claus to buy you new
markers. You need them," said Diane
with a toss of her head.

Sendi ran to the door. She had to
get away from Diane before she did

something bad to her and had one more thing added to the list against her.

Sendi's hand shook as she tried to put the key in the lock. The wind swirled snow around her, and she shivered.

"Here!" said Diane, grabbing the key. "I'll open it for you." She easily unlocked the door and opened it for Sendi. "Here's your key."

Sendi took the key and dropped it in her pocket. "I won't say thank you!" she snapped.

"I don't care," said Diane. "I plan on being nice anyway." She turned and ran to the tree that held her treehouse.

Sendi slammed her door and flung the bag onto the ugly sofa. Running into the kitchen, she jerked open the refrigerator. She drank orange juice right from the pitcher, then put it back. The house was too quiet. She turned on the

TV and let it blare out until there was noise in every corner of the shoebox-sized house.

In her bedroom she saw her Bible on her dresser, and she turned sharply away. She couldn't read her Bible. She couldn't pray.

She clicked off the TV and ran to Gwen's house. Mrs. Lewis opened the door, an afghan in her hand.

"Gwen's practicing her piano and can't have visitors now," said Mrs. Lewis.

Sendi heard the plink, plink of the piano. "It's urgent, Mrs. Lewis," said Sendi, battling her tears. "I have to talk to Gwen right now!"

"Oh, all right, but only for a few minutes." Mrs. Lewis stepped aside, and Sendi dashed past her to the living room.

Gwen turned from the piano in surprise. "What's wrong, Sendi?"

Sendi took a deep breath and said, "Lee will come for Christmas if Mom will let him. She's mad at him and might not let him."

"She won't stay mad," said Gwen, looking very wise. "I have watched my mom and dad have fights and make up. Parents do that."

"I hope you're right."

"I am." Gwen flipped back her hair. "You keep praying and keep loving them both."

Sendi looked down at her feet. "I'll see you later. Come over when you're done practicing."

"I will. Start thinking of a gift you can buy for your parents. I always buy something they can share," said Gwen. "It'll be part of your campaign."

Sendi's head whirled. She'd never

bought anything for Mom to share with someone. What could she buy?

"Last year I bought a picture for their study wall," said Gwen. Her parents had turned one of the bedrooms into a study. They each had a desk and bookcase. They shared a file cabinet, and plants hung near the windows. "Think of something like that."

Sendi nodded. "I'll try." She slowly walked back to her house. Just what could she buy for Mom and Lee together?

Just then the Hansen boys from the house behind Sendi's ran to Sendi's side. Ten-year-old Shawn, the oldest, carried a cardboard box.

"Hi, Sendi," Shawn, Teddy, and Bruce all said at the same time.

Sendi looked at them suspiciously. Sometimes they played tricks on her. "Hi," she said.

"Would you like to buy a wonderful gift for your parents?" asked Teddy who was eight.

Shawn jabbed him in the ribs. "She don't have parents. She has a mom."

Sendi flushed. "Would you like to buy a wonderful gift for your mom?" asked Teddy.

"Our Sunday school class is selling jars of nuts to make some money," said Bruce, the seven-year-old. "Will you buy a jar of nuts?"

"It's a fancy jar," said Shawn as he pulled one out. "See the red ribbon tied around the neck of the jar? See all the nuts? Your mom would love these, wouldn't she?"

Sendi liked the looks of the fancy jar and the nuts inside. "How much does one cost?" she asked.

"Only $8.49," said Teddy.

Sendi had money to spend for

Christmas gifts. But could she spend $8.49 for a jar of nuts? It would be a nice gift for Mom and Lee to share. But it wasn't a "together" gift. Mom could easily pour part of the nuts in another jar and send it home with Lee. Sendi finally shook her head. "I do want to buy something, but not a jar of nuts," she said.

"How about a letter opener?" asked Shawn, digging in his box. "It's made of pewter, and it's real nice."

"You got to watch so you don't stab yourself," said Bruce.

Sendi looked at the letter opener inside the fancy case. A three-masted ship was engraved in a circle on top of the handle. It was beautiful! They couldn't break it apart. It was indeed something to share. Shawn told her the price, and she ran inside to get her money. It took every penny, but she happily took the gift. It was truly a gift for parents to share!

Sendi smiled, suddenly feeling happy again. Just then Diane shouted to Sendi. Sendi's happiness drained away, and she quickly ran inside her house, closed, and locked the door.

7

A Talk with Pine

Sendi raced up the sidewalk to Pine's door. This was the last day of school before Christmas vacation! She'd dropped her bundle of papers and the giant candy bar that had been her gift from Timmy Pelter off at home already. It was only three days until Christmas, and she was sure she'd softened Mom enough that she was ready to let Lee come for Christmas Day.

Sendi knocked on the door, and Pine opened it immediately. He looked strange without his cowboy hat. The scar on the side of his face showed up more.

He laughed down at her. "You look like a girl who just started Christmas vacation," he said, his bright blue eyes twinkling.

"I am!" Sendi cried. Baby mewed, and Sendi picked her up. "You won't have to keep Baby until January third."

"I'll miss her," said Pine, scratching Baby's black and white neck. "You come visit and bring her with you."

Sendi nodded. Pine was like a grandpa to her. Most of the time she liked spending time with him, but now she was afraid he'd see how black her heart was.

"I put up my tree today," said Pine. "Would you like to take a look see?"

Sendi hesitated, then walked after Pine to his living room. The house smelled of peppermint canes and pine. The tree stood in the corner opposite the television. It was covered with red balls and silver tinsel. An angel with wide silver wings and a glistening white gown was at the top. Sendi stepped closer. "It's beautiful, Pine!"

"Your daddy helped me decorate it," said Pine.

"I hope Mom lets him help us," said Sendi with a long sigh.

"You just keep praying for her," said Pine. "For both of them."

Sendi nodded slightly. She'd told Pine about Mom's anger and about her plan to have Lee come for Christmas.

He'd said he'd be praying. She hadn't told him she wasn't really praying for anything because of the sin in her heart.

"Is something wrong, Sendi?" asked Pine softly.

Sendi pushed her face into Baby's hair and shook her head. Oh, she had to get away before he found out more!

Just then someone knocked on Pine's door. Sendi walked with Pine to the door and planned to slip quietly away before Pine could ask any more questions.

Pine opened the door, and Diane Roscommon stood there with a gift in her hand. Sendi jumped back, but not before Diane saw her.

"I brought you this, Pine," said Diane, pushing the gift into his hands.

"Why, thank you, Diane," said Pine, looking down at the gift in surprise.

"Aren't you going to open it?" asked Diane, jumping from one foot to the other.

"I'd rather put it under my tree and open it at Christmas," said Pine.

Diane shrugged. "Okay." She frowned past him at Sendi. "You can't hide from me forever, you know."

Sendi stepped forward with her chin high. "I wasn't hiding from you!"

Diane shrugged, then turned back to Pine. "She's still mad at me. But I plan on being nice to her anyway."

"Is that right," said Pine.

Diane nodded. "We could build a new snowman family together, Sendi," said Diane. "Maybe then you'll get over being mad."

Sendi couldn't look at Pine. Now he'd know how bad she really was!

"She told lies too," said Diane. "She's a bad girl."

Sendi wanted to sink through the floor. Pine slipped an arm around Sendi. "Sendi is a precious girl, Diane. She's going to grow into a mighty woman of God."

"She is?" asked Diane, her eyes wide.

Sendi looked up at Pine in shock. How could he say that about her? She was bad! She was not growing into a mighty woman of God!

"She sure is," said Pine, grinning.

"Then she'd better quit being mad at me," said Diane with a toss of her head. She turned and ran back toward her home.

Pine closed the door, shutting out the cold. He set the gift on the table and turned to Sendi.

She stood with her head down, Baby in her arms.

"I reckon we'd best talk about this," said Pine. "What do you think, Sendi?"

Her eyes brimmed with tears, and she slowly nodded. Pine took Baby and set her on the floor. Then he helped Sendi off with her jacket. He seated her at the tiny round kitchen table, filled a glass with cold water, and handed it to her.

She drank thankfully. The cold water relieved some of the tightness in her throat.

"Now, Sendi girl, tell me what's been goin' on with you and Diane," said Pine as he sat across from her. He folded his work-roughened hands on the table and leaned forward. His skin looked like old leather.

Trembling, Sendi took a deep breath. She started with the snowman family. Little by little, she told Pine everything. She brushed tears off her cheeks as she talked faster and faster. Oh, but it felt good to stop hiding what she'd done! "So, I lied about praying! I couldn't pray!"

Pine took one of Sendi's hands in his. "Jesus loves you, Sendi. He sees your heart. He knows about the anger and the lies."

Sendi bit her lip. Would He stop loving her?

"He still loves you," said Pine.

Sendi breathed a sigh of relief.

"Jesus wants to help you with your problems, but He can't if you don't let Him."

"Would He help get Lee and Mom together so we could be a family?" whispered Sendi.

"He knows what's best for all three of you, and He'll do what is best for you all," said Pine.

"What about . . . Diane?" asked Sendi.

Pine patted Sendi's hand. "You willfully stayed angry at her, and you did lie."

"I know."

"Jesus says if you confess your sins, He will forgive you and cleanse you from all of them." Pine reached across the table and trailed a finger down Sendi's cheek. "It's easy to cut yourself off from God just because you sinned. Never do that! When you sin, run to Him; not away! Let Him take away the sin. It'll set you free to ask for His help."

"Diane is mean!" said Sendi with a break in her voice.

Pine nodded. "I know. But she's learning to let Jesus help her do what's right." Pine leaned back in his chair and folded his hands on the table in front of him. He looked very serious. "Sendi, you can't let what Diane is or is not affect you. You are responsible for your own actions. Diane is responsible for hers. You can't blame Diane for your sins."

"But it was her fault!" cried Sendi.

Pine shook his head. "No, Sendi. Diane was naughty to you, but it wasn't her fault that you did wrong. It was your choice. You knew what God wanted you to do, and you chose not to do it. But now you're ready to make the right choice. You want to ask Jesus to forgive you, and you want to forgive Diane, don't you."

Suddenly Sendi realized she did. It was terrible to carry around the heavy weight she felt inside her! Not being able to pray was terrible. Getting farther and farther away from her Heavenly Father was the worst part. She nodded. "Yes! I am ready!"

Pine walked around and knelt beside her chair. His old bones creaked. "We'll pray right now," he said.

Sendi bowed her head, and she listened as Pine prayed. Then she prayed. Suddenly she felt the heavy black band around her heart snap. Once again she was free! She laughed right out loud and hugged Pine tight.

"Now Jesus can help your family," said Pine.

"Thank You, Jesus," whispered Sendi, her eyes sparkling. Finally Sendi slipped on her jacket and picked up Baby.

"Now I have to talk to Diane," she said with her chin high and her shoulders square.

8

Diane

Sendi took Baby home and then ran to the corner grocery store. The bell tinkled above the door. Sendi smelled dog food and coffee. Mrs. Wells looked up from reading a newspaper behind the cluttered counter. No one else was in the store.

"Hello, Sendi," said Mrs. Wells, smiling.

"I need to ask a favor," said Sendi, lacing her fingers together.

Mrs. Wells shrugged. "Anything, Sendi. You're a good worker."

"I want to buy a pack of magic markers, but I don't have any money. I can work for the markers just like I work for the cat food." Sendi held her breath, waiting for the answer.

Mrs. Wells nodded. "No problem, Sendi. I'll add it to your list."

"Thank you," said Sendi as she hurried to the shelf where the markers hung. She found the pack she wanted, showed them to Mrs. Wells, said goodbye, and ran back home. Cold wind turned her nose and cheeks red.

The next morning after Janice left for work, Sendi wrapped the markers in Christmas paper. She pulled on her snow boots, jacket, warm cap, and fuzzy mittens. She opened the door and blinked in the bright sunlight. Fresh snow had fallen during the night. The tiny front yard was a blanket of snow without a single footprint. It looked almost too clean to walk through, but Sendi ran across to Diane's yard. "Help me, Jesus," whispered Sendi. Butterflies fluttered in her stomach as she knocked on the Roscommons' door.

Diane flung the door wide and smiled at Sendi. "Come in before the house gets cold."

Sendi stepped inside and closed the door. Voices came from the kitchen. The smell of bacon made Sendi's mouth water.

"I knew you wouldn't stay mad forever!" said Diane smugly.

Sendi hesitated, then thrust out the

gift. "This is for you. I'm sorry for lying and for being mad."

Diane ripped off the bright paper and let it fall to the floor. "Markers! Thank you, Sendi! This is great. You can use them any time you want. Just so you don't use 'em up."

"Thanks," said Sendi.

"I've got to finish eating breakfast," said Diane. "See you later."

Sendi smiled and walked back outdoors. She felt as light as a snowflake. She picked up a handful of snow, pressed it into a snowball, and then threw it at the nearby tree. The snowball missed and flew into the street. She laughed and ran into the house to eat breakfast.

Much later she heard a sound in the front yard. She looked out to see Diane rolling a big ball of snow up toward the house. Sendi quickly slipped on her winter gear and ran outside.

"What're you doing, Diane?" asked Sendi.

"Building a snowman family for you," said Diane.

"Thank you!" said Sendi in surprise.

"You can help, you know," said Diane, frowning. "This is cold, hard work."

Sendi scooped up a handful of snow to start the base of another snowman. She rolled the ball across the yard, picking up snow on the ball until it grew so big she could barely roll it.

Just then Gwen ran into the yard. She wore a new pink cap and mittens with her old blue coat. "I saw you from my window," she said. "I came to help."

"Then don't just stand there!" cried Diane as she struggled to lift the middle section of the snowman up onto the bottom section. "I need help!"

Gwen and Sendi ran to Diane and helped lift the middle section in place. Together they worked to smooth out the edges and make a perfect rounded middle section.

Finally they stepped back to admire their work. "This will be a perfect snowman family," said Diane. "This time I won't knock it down."

"Good," said Sendi. Her fingers were wet and cold inside her mittens, but she didn't care. They were going to build a perfect snowman family! Lee would see it, and he'd think about the three of them becoming a perfect family.

Next the girls worked together on the snowman Sendi had started. Suddenly Gwen stopped working. She laughed and jumped high in the air.

"What?" asked Diane, frowning. Her

face was red with cold, and snow clung to her mittens.

Sendi giggled. She was glad to see Gwen happy again. Gwen clapped her hands together, but they they made no sound because of her soggy mittens. "I do have a great mission in life!"

Diane rolled her eyes and went back to work on the snowman.

Sendi gasped, "Does this mean you won't help me with mine?"

Gwen shook her head. "That is my mission in life! Helping others!" Gwen laughed again. She grabbed Sendi and danced her across the snowy yard. Finally she stopped. "Jesus wants us to help others all the time. He wants us to tell others about His love. He wants us to worship God. Just being a Christian gives me a great mission in life!"

Sendi laughed. "It gives all of us a

great mission in life!" That made her feel strange, but glad.

Diane turned with a frown. She stood with her fists jabbed against her thin hips. "Hey, does that even mean me?"

"Yes," said Gwen.

Sendi fell back a step. It was hard to imagine Diane having a great mission in life. Diane always caused so much trouble.

"You're a Christian, Diane," said Gwen. "So it does mean you."

Diane flung her arms wide and shouted at the top of her lungs. She ran to Gwen and hugged her hard. Then she hugged Sendi hard. "I can't believe I actually have a mission in life! Do you know how many times I cried myself to sleep because in my family I'm squished between my brothers and my sisters, and I always felt like a nobody." She twirled around again and shouted again. "I have a reason for being me!"

Sendi thought about that as she looked at the snowman child they'd built. She had come into being because of the terrible mistake Mom and Lee had made, but God still had a special plan for her. He had a mission for her! "I have a reason for being me," she whispered in awe.

9

A Family Christmas

Sendi held the English report to her chest. Could she really read it aloud to Mom to show her how badly she wanted a family Christmas? She heard Mom in the kitchen making Christmas candy.

97

Tomorrow Momma was coming and would stay for three days. Sendi would give Momma her bed, and she'd sleep on the ugly sofa. But Sendi didn't mind a bit. She loved Momma even if she did still try to boss Mom around.

Taking a deep breath, Sendi walked to the kitchen. Mom stood at the table dropping spoonfuls of chocolate candy from a pan onto a piece of waxed paper. The smell of the chocolate filled the room. "Want to read my English assignment, Mom?" Sendi asked as she sat down at the table. She kept the paper pressed to her chest.

Janice looked up with a slight frown. "I'm a little busy right now. What's it about?"

"The title is 'My Favorite Christmas Memory.'"

"That's real nice, Sendi. I never knew you had a favorite memory."

"Do you have one?" asked Sendi.

Janice dropped several more candies on the paper. "Yes, I do! I guess I didn't think I would."

"What was it, Mom?" asked Sendi, leaning forward, eager to hear every word.

Janice spooned more candy out and then set the pan down. She smiled into space. "When I was four years old, Momma and Daddy surprised me with a huge Christmas tree. They knew I wanted a special baby doll. It looked like a real baby. Oh, I wanted a baby sister or brother so badly!"

Sendi knew the feeling.

"So they wrapped the doll up in a special pink baby blanket and tucked it in a little white crib, wrapped it, and then hid it behind the tree." Janice sank to the edge of the chair and smiled dreamily. "Daddy gave me the gifts under the tree that were mine, and I opened them. I was glad for them, but I wanted a baby doll so much that nothing else could really make me happy. Then Daddy told me to reach something behind the tree that he couldn't reach. Momma said to take it out carefully. I crawled under the lowest branch and slowly pulled the gift out." Janice brushed a tear from her eye. "I opened that gift and saw the baby doll, the pink blanket, the little white crib, and I was the happiest little girl alive. Momma and Daddy hugged me and kissed me. I played all day long with that baby doll."

"Whatever happened to it?" asked Sendi softly.

"Momma still has it in her attic. I didn't want to bring it with us until I knew we were settled in our own place.

We aren't going to rent this shoebox for-ever!"

"Did you cry when your daddy left you?" asked Sendi around a lump in her throat.

Janice nodded. "I cried for a long, long time," she whispered.

"Did you love him?"

"I still do."

"I love my dad," said Sendi.

"I know."

"I want my dad here with us."

"Me too, Sendi."

"He said he'd come for Christmas. Can he, Mom?" Sendi sat very still and held her breath.

Janice sighed heavily. Finally she nodded. "He can come."

With a squeal of joy, Sendi ran to Mom and hugged her hard. They weren't a hugging family, but Sendi didn't care. She was so full of love right now, she had to hug Mom or burst. "I love you, Mom!"

"I love you, Sendi," said Janice with a catch in her voice.

"I'll go tell Lee he can come in the morning!" Sendi ran to get her jacket.

"Come right back," said Janice. "He might be going out tonight."

Sendi stiffened. What if he were going out with Lorna Roberts again? Sendi's stomach knotted, and for a minute she couldn't move. Then she shook her head. No, she would not worry about it! She had prayed. God would answer in the very best way.

A few minutes later, she knocked on Pine's door. Lee answered it because Pine was gone. Lee smiled when he saw Sendi. "Come right on in, Sendi," said Lee, catching her hand.

Sendi liked the feel of Lee's hand. She liked the smell of his after-shave.

She squeezed his hand. "Mom says you can come for Christmas! Can you come over for breakfast in the morning and stay all day?"

Lee bent down and hugged Sendi tight. "I'll do just that! Pine will be at his daughter's all day tomorrow, so I'd be all alone."

Sendi stepped back from Lee. She bit her bottom lip. "Lee, are you going to take Lorna Roberts out again?"

Lee shook his head.

"You could take Mom out," said Sendi, watching him. She saw a muscle jump in his cheek.

"She wouldn't go," said Lee, stabbing his fingers nervously through his blond hair.

"She'd go."

"Are you sure?"

Sendi nodded. "We don't want you

going with someone else. We want you for ourselves."

"You do, huh?" Lee chuckled and hugged Sendi again. "Maybe your mom doesn't feel that way."

"She does."

"How do you know?"

"I just know."

"She might not like us talking about this," said Lee. "So you'd better leave this for your mom and me to talk about."

"Okay," said Sendi. "But if you forget, I'll remind you."

Lee playfully tugged Sendi's hair. "You do that. Now you'd better get back home. I'll see you in the morning."

"Momma's coming too," said Sendi.

"I know. I'll be glad to see her. I remember the good cinnamon rolls she used to make."

"She still does," said Sendi. "I'll ask her to make you some."

Lee laughed. "Thanks. Run on home now."

Sendi opened the door. "Are you really glad you're my dad?"

Lee nodded. "Really glad."

Sendi smiled all the way home. The next morning when she opened the door and let Lee in, he had three gifts in his arms. Cold air blew in with him, and Sendi quickly closed the door.

"Who're the presents for?" asked Sendi, barely able to stand still.

Lee winked at Sendi. "For you and your mom and your grandma. Is she here yet?"

"Not yet, but Mom said she'd be here soon. Momma always gets up real early to drive here." Sendi took Lee's coat and hung it in the closet.

"Where's your mom?" asked Lee, looking around the room.

"Changing her clothes again," said Sendi in a low voice. "She didn't like anything she put on. She wants to look pretty for you."

Lee grinned. He walked to the tree. "You did a great job on the tree. It's very pretty."

"I wanted you to help, but Mom was still mad at you," said Sendi.

"I know," said Lee.

Just then Janice walked out of her bedroom. She wore a soft coral jacket and pants. She looked flushed and her eyes sparkled. "Hello, Lee," she said stiffly. Her earrings danced when she moved her head.

"You look beautiful, Mom!" cried Sendi.

"You sure do," said Lee. "Merry Christmas."

"Merry Christmas," said Janice. She pushed her hair back and nervously twisted the ring on her finger. "Did you have breakfast yet?"

Lee shook his head. "No. Did you?"

"No," said Janice. But she didn't move. Sendi had never seen her mom so nervous.

"Then let's go eat," said Sendi, heading for the kitchen.

Sendi watched Mom and Lee as they ate eggs, toast, and bacon. She listened to every word they said, hoping to hear something that would show they were once again falling in love. But they only talked about ordinary stuff.

Later Momma came, and she did most of the talking. She cleaned homes for a living, so she told funny stories about the people she worked for. They all worked in the kitchen to fix Christmas dinner. Sendi stood back and watched. It was almost like her English paper, only better.

While dinner cooked, they sat in the living room on the floor, and Momma sat on the ugly chair as they opened the presents. Sendi liked the sound of the ripping paper and the cries of delight when each person saw the gift. She liked the game of Yahtzee Lee brought her, the winter boots from Momma, and the clothes and books from Mom. Finally only one gift stood under the tree. Sendi trembled as she reached for it.

"This is for my mom and dad," said Sendi as she handed them the present.

Janice and Lee looked at each other. Then Janice took the gift. "We'll both tear off the paper," she said.

Sendi sat in front of them, watching their faces as they opened it.

"A letter opener," said Janice.

"It's beautiful," said Lee as he held it up for Momma to see.

"It is a letter opener," said Momma with a slight frown. "Sendi, you make sure you don't play with that thing. It looks real sharp, and you could stab yourself."

"Oh, Momma, she won't," said Janice as she put the opener back in the box. "Thank you, Sendi. It's a pretty gift."

"It's for both of you together," said Sendi.

"Thank you," said Janice, blushing to the roots of her blonde hair.

"Thank you," said Lee, looking at the pile of torn wrapping paper.

Momma pushed herself up. She tugged her blue big shirt over her navy slacks. "Well, I'm ready for another cup of coffee. Sendi, come sit with me while I drink it."

Sendi wanted to stay and watch Mom and Lee, but she followed Momma to the kitchen.

Momma poured herself a cup of coffee and added a little sugar and milk. She sat down and picked up a cookie she'd brought. "I saw your snowmen out front, Sendi."

"It's a family," said Sendi proudly.

"I guessed it was." Momma studied Sendi thoughtfully. "You got your heart set on your mom and Lee getting married, don't you?"

"Yes," whispered Sendi. Her nerves tightened, and her stomach knotted painfully.

"Don't get your hopes too high, Sendi," said Momma.

"I won't," said Sendi. "I prayed and I know God will answer."

"What if He answers differently than you want?"

Sendi locked her hands in her lap. "I know God will answer best for all of us," she said around the lump in her throat.

A week later Sendi watched out the window as Mom and Lee walked to his car to go on a real date. Pine was baby-sitting her. Smiling until she thought her face would break, Sendi turned to him. "They're going to dinner."

Pine leaned back in the ugly chair and grinned. "I know."

Sendi twirled around the room and then dropped to the ugly sofa. "They'll get engaged, then get married, then live happily ever after."

For two months Sendi waited for Mom to say they were going to get married, but neither Mom nor Lee said a word. Every day Sendi talked to Gwen about her wonderful dream about being a family. Sometimes Sendi even talked to Diane about her dream. For once Diane didn't make fun of her or say it couldn't happen. All three girls prayed about it every day.

One night in March Mom sent Sendi over to Gwen's to watch a video so she and Lee could be alone to talk. Afterward she ran home through the icy wind and shivered as she opened her back door. The heat of the kitchen wrapped around her. The room smelled of coffee and pizza. Music drifted in from the living room.

Sendi ran to the doorway and then stopped short. Lee and Mom were standing in the middle of the room with their arms around each other. They were kissing just like people did on TV. Sendi giggled.

Lee looked up. He winked at Sendi. Then he came over, caught her hands, and danced her around the small room.

Stopping beside Janice, he announced, "Sendi, I asked your mom if she'd marry me."

Sendi squealed in delight.

Janice laughed happily. "And I said yes!" She held her left hand out to Sendi. A small diamond ring sparkled on her finger. "See my beautiful ring?"

Sendi held Mom's hand and admired the ring. Tears of happiness filled Sendi's eyes, and she couldn't speak.

Lee sat down on the edge of the sofa and pulled Sendi to him. "Sendi Lee Mason, may I marry your mom?"

Sendi looked from Mom to Lee and back again. "Yes! Oh, yes!" she cried.

10

A Real Family

Sendi paced the living room. Where was Mom? She had promised to be home right on time so they could go shopping. Today was the day Sendi was buying her dress for the wedding! She laughed. God had answered her prayer even better than she'd imagined. On

April 6 Lee and Mom were going to get married. Sendi was to be junior bridesmaid, and Pine was giving the bride away.

Just then Gwen knocked and walked in. "Sendi, I just heard something terrible!"

Sendi shivered. "What?"

"That you're moving!"

Sendi fell back a step and bumped into the ugly chair. "No! What do you mean?"

"Your mom told mine that you'd be moving," said Gwen close to tears. "I heard Mom telling Dad. Then they shut their study door, and I couldn't hear anything more."

Sendi's legs gave way, and she dropped to the edge of the chair. "Mom has been acting so funny lately. Maybe she called off the wedding. Maybe we're going back to live with Momma!"

"Oh, Sendi! That would be devastating!" Gwen sank down on the ugly sofa. "Who would be my very best friend?"

"If we are going to move, maybe it means Mom and Lee aren't going to get married." Sendi burst into tears. Then from deep inside she remembered God was answering her prayer. She could not give up now even if things looked bad. She lifted her head and wiped away her tears. "I will not cry, Gwen! Remember, God is with us and working out things for our best."

Gwen jumped up. "You're right, Sendi. You just better not be moving out of Greenlea!"

Sendi looked around at the shoe-box-sized house. They'd lived in it almost a year. She'd gotten used to it. But it would be very small for three people.

Just then Janice ran into the

house. She looked flushed and happy. "I brought the perfect dress home for you, Sendi!" Janice smiled at Gwen. "Hi. Would you like to see Sendi try on her dress?"

"Oh, yes!" cried Gwen.

Sendi ran after Mom to the bedroom where Mom pulled the dress from the box. Sendi gasped. The dress was her very favorite shade of blue, and it had long sleeves and a flared skirt.

"It's too beautiful for words," said Gwen.

"I love it, Mom!" whispered Sendi, touching the soft fabric.

"It'll look great on you," said Gwen. Sendi quickly pulled off her jeans and sweater and slipped on her dress. It fit just right. It would be perfect with her new shoes. "It's so pretty I don't want to take it off."

"You have to," said Janice, laughing

breathlessly. "Lee will be here in a few minutes, and we have a great surprise for you."

Sendi and Gwen exchanged glances. "You may go with us if you want, Gwen," said Janice.

"I can't," said Gwen with a long sigh. "Dad said I have to stay home."

"Sendi will come see you when we return," said Janice.

Sendi's stomach fluttered. It was hard not to ask a million questions.

A couple of minutes later, Gwen walked out just as Lee arrived. He wore a tan spring jacket, western shirt, and jeans. He hugged Sendi and gave Janice a long kiss. Sendi smiled so hard her mouth felt as if it would crack. She loved seeing Lee kiss Mom.

"Are you girls ready?" asked Lee, winking at Sendi.

"Ready," said Janice breathlessly.

"Where're we going?" asked Sendi.

"You'll see," said Lee and Janice together. Sendi followed them to Lee's car. A dog barked across the street, and a robin landed in the yard, then flew away. The spring breeze felt good against Sendi's flushed face.

Lee turned the car out of the driveway, past Pine's house to Langston Street, then went left. Almost immediately he turned left again into a long driveway.

"Here we are," said Lee.

"Where?" asked Sendi. She knew Amy Vandecar once lived in the big white house with the big yard. She'd moved away just after Christmas.

Janice laughed as she slipped from the car. She waited until Sendi stood beside her. "This is our home," said Janice proudly as she waved her arm in an arc to take in the yard, the house, and the garage. "We no longer have to rent that shoebox! We are buying this house!"

Sendi gasped. Was this a dream? But she knew the line of trees between this yard and Pine's was real. She could see Gwen's backyard. Camille was walking to the back door with her tail high in the air. A squirrel chattered up in a tree. Yes, this was real!

"It has four bedrooms," said Lee as he slipped an arm around Janice. "We wanted something big enough for a family. In a couple of years you'll have a brother or sister, Sendi."

Sendi bit her lip to keep from crying for joy. God had answered even better than she'd dreamed possible!

"Let's look inside," said Lee, pulling the key from his pocket.

Sendi followed them in. The house was totally empty, and their voices echoed, but Sendi could picture how it would look with furniture and pictures on the wall.

"Here's the bedroom I thought you'd like," said Janice as they walked into a room almost as big as the whole shoebox house.

Sendi looked at the two tall windows and the giant closet. She ran to a window and looked out right on Gwen's house. Sendi ran back and hugged Janice. "Thanks, Mom." Sendi hugged Lee. "Thanks, Lee."

Lee bent down to Sendi. "I'm your dad, Sendi. Can you please call me Dad?"

Sendi laughed and nodded. "Dad." She rolled the wonderful word around on her tongue. "*Dad!*"

On April 6 Sendi walked down the church aisle dressed in her blue dress and carrying one red rose. Her stomach fluttered nervously, but she walked just as she'd practiced. Lee smiled at her from where he stood with the pastor.

Finally the music swelled, and it was time for Janice. She stepped through the doors with her arm through Pine's. He looked proud, but uncomfortable in a dark blue suit. Janice wore a long white wedding gown with a veil over her face. She looked so beautiful Sendi almost cried. She glanced at Lee. He had tears in his eyes, but he was smiling.

Finally Pine handed Janice over to Lee, and they stood before the pastor and said their vows. Sendi glanced at Gwen and smiled. Sendi was going to stay with Gwen while Mom and Dad went on their honeymoon.

At the end of the ceremony, the pastor said in his ringing voice, "I'm proud to present to you Mr. and Mrs. Lee Reins."

Sendi smiled as her parents looked out at the guests. They clapped and shouted, then grew quiet.

"Sendi," said the pastor. Sendi stiffened. This had not been in the practice! "Come here, Sendi," said the pastor softly. Slowly Sendi walked to him. He took her hand and then handed her over to Lee and Janice.

The pastor said, "Greet this wonderful new family. Lee, Janice, and Sendi Reins!"

Beaming happily, Sendi looked up at Dad, then at Mom. They smiled down at her and then bent down and kissed her cheeks. Together they marched down the aisle and out of the church. Sendi took her place beside Mom in the receiving line just as they'd practiced.

Sendi's heart swelled with joy as

she waited for Momma to reach her side and stand beside her to greet the guests.